Geraldine, the Music Mouse

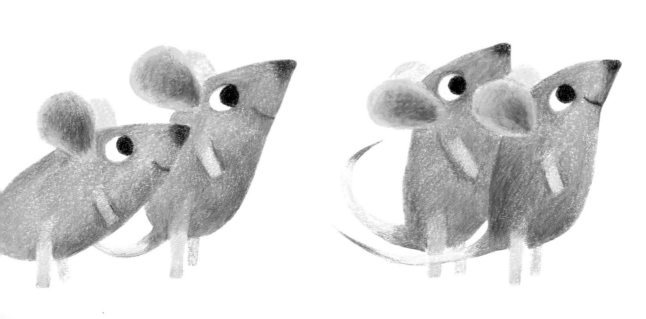

Leo Lionni

Geraldine, the Music Mouse

Dragonfly Books —— New York

Geraldine had never heard music before. Noises, yes.
Many noises—the voices of people, the slamming of doors,
the barking of dogs, the rushing of water, the meows
of cats in the courtyard. And, of course, the soft peeping of
mice. But music, never.
    Then one morning . . .

In the pantry of the empty house where Geraldine
lived, she discovered an enormous piece of Parmesan
cheese—the largest she had ever seen. Eagerly, she took
a little bite from it. It was delicious. But how would she be
able to take it to her secret hideout in the barn?

She ran to her friends who lived next door and told them about her discovery.

"If you help me carry it to my hideout," she said, "I'll give each of you a big piece."

Her friends, who loved cheese, happily agreed.

"Let's go!" they said. And off they went.

"It's enormous! It's gigantic! It's immense! It's fantastic!"
they shouted with joy when they saw the piece of cheese.

They pushed and pulled and tugged and finally they managed to carry it to Geraldine's hideout.

There, Geraldine climbed to the very top of the
cheese. She dug her little teeth into it and pulled away
crumb after crumb, chunk after chunk.

As her friends carried away their cheese tidbits, Geraldine peered in amazement at the hole she had gnawed. There she saw the shapes of two enormous ears—cheese ears!

As soon as her friends were gone, she went back to work again, nibbling away at the cheese as fast as she could. When she was halfway through, Geraldine climbed down to have a look at the forms she had freed. She could hardly believe what she saw. The ears were those of a giant mouse, still partly hidden, of solid cheese. To its puckered lips it held a flute. Geraldine gnawed and gnawed until she had finally uncovered the entire mouse.

Then she realized that the flute was really the tip
of the mouse's tail. Astonished, exhausted, and a little
frightened, Geraldine stared at the cheese statue.
With the dimming of the last daylight, she fell asleep.

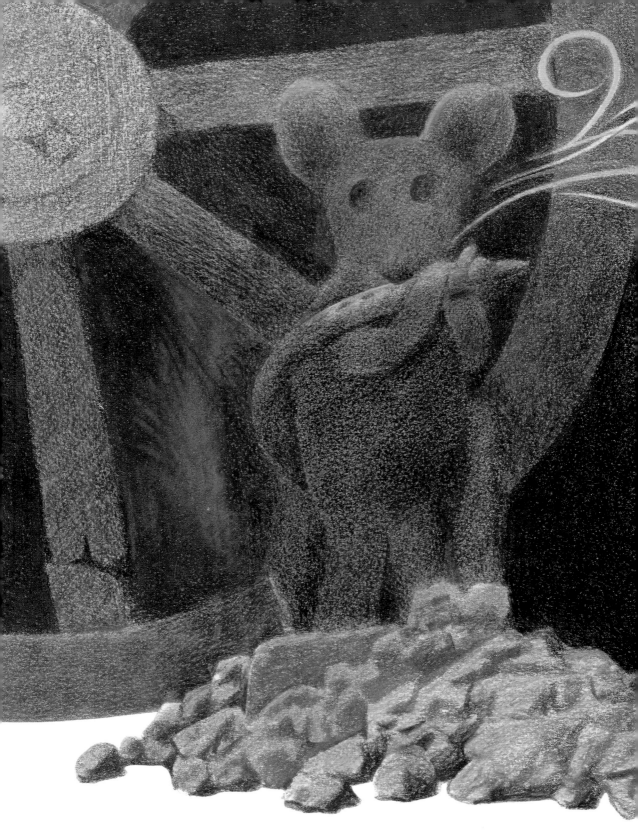

Suddenly she was awakened by some strange sounds. They seemed to come from the direction of the mouse's flute. She jumped to her feet. As it grew darker, the sounds became clearer and more melodious until they seemed to move lightly through the air like invisible strings of silver and gold. Never had Geraldine heard anything so beautiful.

"Music!" she thought. "This must be music!"

She listened all through the night until the first glow of dawn filtered through the dusty windowpanes.

But as the cheese mouse was slowly bathed in light, the music became softer, until it stopped altogether.

"Play, play," Geraldine begged. "Play some more!"

But not a sound came from the flute.

"Will it ever play again?" Geraldine thought as she gobbled up some of the crumbs that lay around.

When the next evening approached, it brought the answer to her question. The music began faintly at dusk and lasted until the break of day. And so, night after night, the cheese flutist played for Geraldine. She learned to recognize the melodies, and even in daylight they lingered in her ears.

Then one day she met her friends on the street.
They were desperate.

"Geraldine!" they said. "We have no more food,
and there is none to be found anywhere. You
must share your cheese with us."

"But that is not possible!" Geraldine shouted.
"Why?" asked the others, angrily.
"Because . . . because . . . because it is MUSIC!"
Her friends looked at Geraldine, surprised.
"What is music?" they asked all together.

For a moment Geraldine stood deep in thought. Then she took a step backward, solemnly lifted the tip of her tail to her puckered lips, took a deep breath and blew. She blew hard. She puffed, she peeped, she tweeted, she screeched. Her friends laughed until their hungry little tummies hurt.

Then a long, soft, beautiful whistle came from Geraldine's lips. One of the melodies of the cheese flute echoed in the air. The little mice held their breath in amazement. Other mice came to hear the miracle. When the tune came to an end, Gregory, the oldest of the group, whispered, "If this is music, Geraldine, you are right. We cannot eat that cheese."

"No," said Geraldine, joyfully. "Now we CAN eat the cheese. Because . . . now the music is in me."

With that they all followed Geraldine to the barn.

And while Geraldine whistled the gayest of tunes, they ate cheese to their tummies' content.

All rights reserved. Published in the United States by Dragonfly Books,
an imprint of Random House Children's Books, a division of Random House, Inc., New York.
Originally published in hardcover in the United States by Pantheon Books,
a division of Random House, Inc., New York, in 1979.

Dragonfly Books with the colophon is a registered trademark of Random House, Inc.

Visit us on the Web! www.randomhouse.com/kids

Educators and librarians, for a variety of teaching tools,
visit us at www.randomhouse.com/teachers

The Library of Congress has cataloged the hardcover edition of this work as follows:
Lionni, Leo.
Geraldine, the music mouse / Leo Lionni.
p. cm.
Summary: After nibbling an enormous piece of parmesan cheese into the shape of
a giant mouse holding a flute, Geraldine hears music for the first time.
ISBN: 978-0-394-84238-7 (trade) — ISBN: 978-0-394-94238-4 (lib. bdg.)
[1. Music—Fiction. 2. Mice—Fiction.] I. Title.
PZ7.L6634G
[E] 79000932

ISBN: 978-0-375-85514-6 (pbk.)

MANUFACTURED IN CHINA

10 9 8 7 6 5 4 3 2 1
First Dragonfly Books Edition